Rhymes 'n Rhythms

for the ESL classroom

Lisa Tenuta

Pro Lingua Associates

Pro Lingua Associates, Publishers
P.O.Box 1348
Brattleboro, Vermont 05302 USA

Office: 802 257 7779
Orders: 800 366 4775
Fax: 802 257 5117
E-mail: prolingu@sover.net
www.ProLinguaAssociates.com
SAN: 216-0579

*At **Pro Lingua***
our objective is to foster an approach
to learning and teaching that we call
***interplay,** the **inter**action of language*
learners and teachers with their materials,
with the language and culture,
and with each other in active, creative,
*and productive **play.***

ISBN 0-86647-133-2

Teachers may photocopy the rhymes in this book for classroom use only.

A cassette with readings of the rhymes in this book is available.

This book was designed and set by Arthur A. Burrows using the Baskerville typeface with Monotype Corsiva display. This Baskerville is a modern digital revival of the neoclassic monotype face designed by John Baskerville in Birmingham, England, in the 1750's; it was a great favorite of Baskerville's contemporary, printer Benjamin Franklin, who introduced it to the United States, where it has been a standard face ever since. Corsiva is a widely used digital adaptation of a monotype display face notable for its strong rhythmical elements. The book was printed and bound by Capital City Press in Montpelier, Vermont.

Printed in the United States of America
First printing 2000. 3000 copies.

For my brother, Brad

Special thanks to Ray Clark for all the time he spent tapping out the rhymes, to the students at Desert View High School in Tucson, Arizona, who practiced them, and to my husband, Joe, who was always willing to listen to them.

Vowel Symbols and Sounds Used in This Book

Symbol	Sound
/a/	pot
/ay/	pie
/aw/	paw
/ar/	part
/æ/	pat
/e/	pet
/ey/	pay
/eyr/	pair
/er/	per
/i/	pit
/iy/	Pete
/iyr/	peer
/o/	boat
/oy/	boy
/ow/	bout
/or/	bore
/u/	book
/uw/	boot
/ə/	but

Contents

Contents

Introduction

This is a photocopyable collection of rhythmic rhymes for learners of English at the beginning level, although many of them can also be used quite successfully with intermediate and even advanced learners. The collection can be used selectively with young learners and in its entirety with young adults and adults. The rhymes are very rhythmic, and may be used chorally in class in a variety of enjoyable ways to introduce, review, or just have fun with pronunciation, vocabulary, and grammar.

Speaking with the natural rhythm of English is not easy for many language learners because English is a rather unusual language that has a stress-timed rhythmic pattern. Stressed syllables are spoken louder and longer than unstressed syllables, which tend to collapse and even disappear. For example, "Where did you go?" (four syllables) becomes "Wherdjago?" (three syllables) in naturally spoken English, with only "where" and "go" spoken loudly and clearly. Saying and chanting these rhymes is an excellent way of illustrating and practicing the stress-timed rhythm of English with its accompanying **reduction** and **elision** of sounds and syllables. The first selection in the book following this introduction, *A Practice Rhythm*, is very regular in its rhythmic pattern and contains very easy vocabulary. It can be used to introduce the students to saying the rhymes in rhythmic unison.

Rhymes said aloud will also be useful for working on the basic statement and question **intonation** patterns. The rhymes also call attention to the pronunciation of individual vowel sounds. An accompanying cassette is available to use as a model for the pronunciation of individual words and the rhythmic patterns of the rhymes.

New **vocabulary** will undoubtedly be encountered in the rhymes, but with a few exceptions, most of the words are within Pro Lingua's 600-word beginner level.* Those words that do not occur in the 600-word level are noted on the Notes page as "Lexical Challenges." Note also that, in general, the vocabulary in the rhymes is more challenging in the later parts of the collection.

* The 600 words in ***The Learner's Lexicon***, to be published in 2001, are words that a beginner should know.

Basic English **grammatical structures** occur repetitively throughout the rhymes. The learners will encounter sentence word order, verb phrases with auxiliaries, simple tenses, imperatives, and noun phrases with determiners, adjectives, and plural forms.

On the next page a **Basic Procedure** for teaching the rhymes is described. Although teachers are encouraged to use the rhymes in ways that make sense in their own teaching context, in general the basic procedure works very well in most situations and is the best way to begin using the rhymes. The basic procedure will work equally well with all the rhymes in this collection.

There is a **NOTES** page facing each rhyme. This page contains the following three sections:

Additional Activities. In addition to the basic procedure, these activities offer various additional ways for using the rhyme and exploring and expanding on the linguistic and topical content of the rhymes.

Linguistic Notes. These notes summarize the grammatical and phonological content of the rhymes. They will be useful for correlating the rhymes with other classroom work on grammar and pronunciation. The rhyming vowel sounds in each selection are summarized in these linguistic notes so that special attention can be paid to the pronunciation of the vowels in the rhyme.

Lexical Challenges. As mentioned before, most of the words in the rhymes are familiar to the beginning-level student. However, some may be new, and attention should be paid to unfamiliar vocabulary. Obviously, it is impossible to predict with great accuracy what will be known by any group or individual learner. However, the words cited as "lexical challenges" are words that are not within the 600-word level in Pro Lingua's ***The Learner's Lexicon***. Therefore, there is a high probability that they will be unfamiliar to the beginning-level student.

Although the rhymes afford lots of opportunities for exploring and practicing English pronunciation, vocabulary, and grammar, it is important to remember that the reading, saying, and chanting should also be enjoyable. This material exemplifies Pro Lingua's guiding principle, **interplay** – the **inter**action of language learners and teachers with their materials, with the language and culture, and with each other in active, creative, and productive **play.**

Basic Procedure

Each of the rhymes has additional activities that will be helpful in getting the most out of the time spent with the rhymes. There are, of course, many other ways to use these rhymes, and teachers should adapt their teaching to the specifics of their teaching context. The basic procedure outlined below will, however, work in most teaching situations and can be used with all the rhymes in the collection.

1. Make photocopies of the rhyme.

2. Read the entire rhyme once through aloud to the class, or play the recorded version of the rhyme. This gives a general idea of the theme and the sound of the rhyme. You may want the students to follow along with a copy of the rhyme, or withhold the copy for the next step so that they focus on the sound and not on the shape of the words and lines.

3. Go through the rhyme line by line for comprehension. At this point, it is usually best for the students to have a copy of the rhyme so they may follow along and make notes. You can identify the new words and put them on the board or poster paper or an overhead. Ask the students to guess the meanings of the new words.

4. Read the rhyme a second time, perhaps a little slower, snapping your fingers or tapping out the rhythm as the students listen.

5. Read the rhyme again to the class with the students tapping. This helps them establish a feel for the rhythm.

6. Divide the class in half, or some other grouping. Have the groups take turns saying and listening to the rhyme. This often works better than having the entire class say every line, because the first few readings can be rough, noisy, and difficult to control. To help the reading go smoother, it is often better for you to lead the chorus at this step.

7. Have the entire class say the entire rhyme without you, although you could keep the rhythm flowing by tapping.

8. Individuals can volunteer to say all or parts of the rhyme.

NOTES FOR *A Practice Rhyme*

This practice rhyme should be used to introduce the students to saying lines in unison, and with the appropriate stress-timed rhythm of English. Because this could be the first rhyme you use, it is advisable to follow the basic procedure on the previous page.

ADDITIONAL ACTIVITIES

1. Assign the pronouns to different individuals or pairs (one student/pair for all three third-person forms). The whole class says the last line. For example:

Student A:	I sing.
Student B:	You sing.
Student C:	He, she, it sings.
Student D:	We sing.
Student E:	They sing.
Class:	All the pretty birds sing.

   Note that the second and fourth verses are said with the pronouns in the reverse order.

2. Ask the students to rewrite the rhyme with verbs of their own. They may have to change the last line to have the rhyme make sense. One-syllable verbs work best, for example (irregulars) *come, fall, fly, grow, hear, know, leave, read, run, see, speak, stand, teach, tell, think, write;* (regulars) *ask, care, cook, count, cry, dance, dream, help, hope, laugh, move, play, point, stop, talk, try, wait, watch.*

3. Make a three-column list of the third person singular ending sounds:

	/s/	/z/	/iz/
ex:	walks	sings	teaches

   Have the students put the other verbs they know in the proper column, as in the examples.

LINGUISTIC NOTES

1. This rhyme practices the conjugation of the simple present. It can also be done in the past tense to practice regular and irregular verb forms.

2. The rhythm is extremely simple and regular throughout, following this pattern:

```
/    /
/    /
/    /    /    /
/    /
/    /
/_   /_   /    /
```

   Notice the reduction of the second and fourth syllables of the last line. Be sure the students make these reductions.

LEXICAL CHALLENGES
active   smiling   deep

A Practice Rhyme

I sing.
You sing.
He, she, it sings.
We sing.
They sing.
All the pretty birds sing.

They walk.
We walk.
He, she, it walks.
You walk.
I walk.
All the active boys walk.

I go.
You go.
He, she, it goes.
We go.
They go.
All the smiling girls go.

They sit.
We sit.
He, she, it sits.
You sit.
I sit.
All the tired dogs sit.

I sleep.
You sleep.
He, she, it sleeps.
We sleep.
They sleep.
Close your eyes for deep sleep.

Rhymes 'n Rhythms

NOTES FOR *Questions, Questions*

ADDITIONAL ACTIVITIES 1.1

1. In pairs, the students ask each other and answer all the questions in the rhyme. They answer using complete sentences. If an answer is negative, they should respond with an alternative idea. For example:

A: Do you like reading a good mystery?

B: No, I don't like mysteries. I like to read romance stories.

2. Read the rhyme once aloud to the students. Then have the students read the rhyme by themselves and number each stanza 1-5. Have the students turn their papers over. Then read the rhyme again aloud with the stanzas scrambled. As you read, the students write (or call out) the correct stanza number. You can also copy, cut, and paste a scrambled version and hand it out.

LINGUISTIC NOTES

1. There are all types of questions in this rhyme:
   - — question words: how, where, what
   - — yes/no questions: Do you want to play the question game?
   - — *be* alternative questions: Is it blue or is it gray?
   - — negative questions: Isn't English fun to take?
   - — questions with modals: Would you like a little more? Will you practice every part?
2. Question intonation can be practiced. Normal wh-question intonation falls at the end of the sentence, whereas, normal yes/no intonation rises.
3. There are four stressed syllables in each line, resulting in considerable reduction and elision through out the rhyme.
4. Rhyming vowel sounds in this rhyme are:

/ey/—name, game, today, gray, take, break
/iy/ — tea, mystery
/u/ — book, cook
/aw/ — wall, fall
/or/ — door, floor
/o/ — poem, home (not an exact rhyme)
/ar/ — part, heart

LEXICAL CHALLENGES

cook	mystery	wall	floor	fun
repeat	poem	twice	by heart	

Questions, Questions

1.1

How do you do? And how are you?
I speak English. How about you?
Where are you from? And what's your name?
Do you want to play the question game?

What do you like? Do you like books?
What can you do? Do you like to cook?
What do you like, coffee or tea?
Do you like reading a mystery?

What's the weather like today?
Is it blue or is it gray?
See the sun upon the wall.
Is it winter, spring, or fall?

Is there someone at the door?
Is there something on the floor?
Isn't English fun to take?
And what do you do when you take a break?

Would you please repeat this poem?
Say it twice and then go home.
Will you practice every part
until you learn it all by heart?

NOTES FOR *Only Questions, Please*

ADDITIONAL ACTIVITIES 1.2

1. Divide the class into two groups. Assign each group two lines from each stanza. Practice the rhyme a few times, assigning the lines differently each time. For example, one group reads lines 1 and 2 from each stanza; the other reads lines 3 and 4. Try other variations.
2. Copy the rhyme without the pronouns. Read it aloud and have the students fill in the missing pronouns.
3. Copy the rhyme without the pronouns. Ask the students in pairs to fill in the blanks with pronouns of their own choosing, making all the necessary changes. Then have the eachpair read their rhymes to another pair.

LINGUISTIC NOTES

1. All the questions are yes/no questions, and therefore, end with rising intonation.
2. There are three types of subject-verb inversions in these questions:
   Auxiliary DO + SUBJ + V — Do you have
   BE + SUBJ — Is it
   Auxiliary MODAL + SUBJ + V — May I take
3. All of the subject pronouns are used in this rhyme.
4. The shortened question lines such as "May I? Is it? Does it? Do we? Can he? Will he? Was it?" provide good practice with the linking of the two words. Also note the elision of the /h/ in "Can he?" and "Will he?"
5. Be sure the students practice reduction of unstressed syllables, as in "DO ya HAVE a BOOK?" and "DO ya, DO ya, DO ya."
6. Rhyming vowel sounds are:

   /u/ — book, look
   /æ/ — cat, fat
   /uw/ — school, pool
   /ay/ — rhyme, time, lines
   /ə/ — done, fun

LEXICAL CHALLENGES

fat pool rhyme lines

Only Questions, Please

1.2

Do you have a book?
Do you? Do you? Do you?
May I take a look?
May I? May I? May I?

Does she have a cat?
Does she? Does she? Does she?
Is it big and fat?
Is it? Is it? Is it?

Do they go to school?
Do they? Do they? Do they?
Does it have a pool?
Does it? Does it? Does it?

Do we like this rhyme?
Do we? Do we? Do we?
Do we say it all the time?
Do we? Do we? Do we?

Can he say this rhyme?
Can he? Can he? Can he?
Will he say the lines?
Will he? Will he? Will he?

Is our rhyme all done?
Is it? Is it? Is it?
Was it lots of fun?
Was it? Was it? Was it?

NOTES FOR *Who, What, When, Where, Why, and How*

ADDITIONAL ACTIVITIES 1.3

1. Give one group the third stanza. The other group has stanzas 1 and 2. Everybody says stanza 4. The reading goes like this: stanzas 3 - 1 - 3 - 2 - 3 - 4.
2. The students underline each question word in the rhyme. Then they write an original question for each question word. Finally, in pairs, groups, or as a class, they ask and answer each other's questions.
3. Cut the rhyme into strips, one for each line. Give the strips to different students. Read the rhyme a few times, and then have the students say it using their strip in the correct sequence. Keep trying until the class can do it perfectly.
4. Have the students brainstorm other animal names. Each student chooses an animal and writes a wh-question about that animal on a slip of paper, for example: "Where do crocodiles live?" Collect the slips, mix them up, and hand them out. For homework the students have to answer the question.
5. Assign the question words to different students. As the class reads the rhyme without saying the question words, the students with question words say them at the right time.

For example:	Student A:	Who? Who? Who?
	Class:	Said the owl to the gnu.
	Student B:	What?
	Student C:	When?
	Student D:	Where?
	Class:	Said the monkey to the bear.

LINGUISTIC NOTES

1. Have the students notice the use of quotation marks.
2. The word order of "X, said the Y," rather than "the Y said X" is unusual in speech. The students can write out and practice saying both patterns:
   "Who?" said the owl to the gnu. — The owl said "Who?" to the gnu.
3. The first two stanzas have a different metric pattern from the second two stanzas. The transition may take a little practice.
4. Rhyming vowel sounds are:
   /uw/ — who, gnu
   /ow/ — how, cow
   /eyr/ — where, bear, there
   /ey/ — day, say
   /ay/ — why, fly, try — also note *tiger* and *lion*

LEXICAL CHALLENGES owl monkey gnu bear tiger fly lion cow fun

Who, What, When, Where, Why, and How

1.3

"Who? Who? Who?"
said the owl to the gnu.
"What? When? Where?"
said the monkey to the bear.

"Why? Why? Why?"
said the tiger to the fly.
"How? How? How?"
said the lion to the cow.

Questions here and questions there.
Questions, questions everywhere.
So ask a question every day,
and this is what you have to say:

Who and what and when and where.
Ask a question anywhere.
Where and when and how and why.
Question words are fun to try.

NOTES FOR *Questions and Answers*

ADDITIONAL ACTIVITIES 1.4

1. Divide the class into sections and give each section a different part of the rhyme. Some sections can have questions and the other sections can have answers. Practice saying the rhyme without losing the rhythm.
2. Have the students choose one question from each stanza and write 4-5 answers for it.
3. Ask each student to write 4-5 sentences about what they are doing right now. Then the students look around the classroom and describe what their classmates are doing.
4. The students think of a family member or friend and describe what they think that person is doing.
5. Write several well-known local location names on the board and have the students write sentences or short paragraphs describing what is going on there.

LINGUISTIC NOTES

1. The rhyme offers plenty of practice with pronoun and verb agreement with the auxiliary BE. Some of the forms are contracted, but as the rhyme becomes familiar to the students, all of them can be practiced in contracted, elided speech, for example: what is — what's.
2. The present progressive is practiced throughout this rhyme.
3. Notice "They're having some lunch." The main verb "have" is usually a stative verb and is not used in the present progressive. However, in this case, with the meaning of *enjoy* or *experience*, it can be used in the progressive.
4. Rhyming vowel sounds are:
   /aw/ — song, long
   /o/ — Rome, home
   /ə/ — lunch, munch

LEXICAL CHALLENGES

party whole flying munch

Questions and Answers

1.4

What is she doing?
She's studying English.
What is he doing?
He's singing a song.
What are they doing?
They're having a party.
They're having a party the whole night long.

Where are you going?
I'm going to London.
Where are we going?
We're going to Rome.
Where is she going?
She's going to Paris.
She's going to Paris and then flying home.

NOTES FOR *Around the World*

ADDITIONAL ACTIVITIES 2.1

1. Before reading the rhyme, ask the students to name their favorite city. Have them write three things they like about it.
2. Read or play the rhyme once, and then practice saying the names of the cities.
3. Have the students locate the cities on a map and name the countries they're in.
4. Ask the students to write answers to each of the "Name three things. . ." lines. On large sheets of paper or on the blackboard write headings for the key word (*blue, yellow, pretty,* etc.), and have the students write their answers under the appropriate key word. Check the spelling and clarify the vocabulary.
5. In groups, the students make up new "Name three things..." lines. The groups can then quiz each other on their lines. For example, group one asks group two to name three sports. Group two gets a point for every correct answer.
6. Also see 2.2 "Loads of Languages" for more country names.

LINGUISTIC NOTES

1. The /th/ sound occurs repeatedly (three, things, think) in this rhyme. It's a good opportunity to practice it.
2. Work on stress placement with the pronunciation of the cities. Have the students divide each name into syllables, for example, A-bu-Dha-bi. Then have them mark or highlight the heaviest stressed syllable in each name.
3. Rhyming vowel sounds are:

    /uw/ – Timbuktu, blue
    /iy/ – Aberdeen, green, Tripoli, "t"
    /o/ – Portobello, yellow, Tokyo, know, Rome, poem
    /i/ – Ci̲ty, pre̲tty, Ladyvi̲lle, grill
    /ə/ – Edmonton, fun
    /or/ – Salvador, store

LEXICAL CHALLENGES

All place names *Note:* Ladyville is in Belize.

name cook grill sports fun grocery store vegetables poem

Around the World

2.1

Abu Dhabi, Timbuktu.
Name three things that are colored blue.

Paris, London, Aberdeen.
Name three things that are colored green.

Quito, Bangkok, Portobello.
Name three things that are colored yellow.

Haifa, Cairo, New York City.
Name three things that you think are pretty.

Tucson, Dakar, Ladyville.
Name three things that you cook on a grill.

Cancun, Moscow, Tripoli.
Name three things that end with "t."

Peking, Athens, Edmonton.
Name three sports that you think are fun.

Delhi, Perth, San Salvador.
Name three things in a grocery store.

Hong Kong, Lima, Tokyo.
Name three vegetables that you know.

Dresden, Hanoi, Windhoek, Rome.
Say three things to end this poem.

NOTES FOR *Loads of Languages*

ADDITIONAL ACTIVITIES 2.2

1. Have the students name the languages they speak and say a few words for the others in the class. Have everyone say and write on the board "Welcome to __language__."
2. After saying or playing the rhyme once, ask the students to identify the country where the language is spoken. Locate the countries on a map.
3. Use the previous rhyme, "Around the World," and have the students try to name the languages spoken in those cities.

LINGUISTIC NOTES

1. Speakers of many languages have trouble with /l/ sounds, and there are lots of /l/ sounds in this rhyme. Here is some good practice. Begin with the title and have the students practice saying it. After practicing the title, locate the other words with /l/ and underline or highlight them.
2. Identify the person noun for each language, for example, "A _____ speaks English." Latin, of course, doesn't have speakers, unless you say, "Romans spoke Latin."
3. You can do some work with the /sh/ and /ch/ distinction, although there lots of /sh/ sounds, there are only three /ch/ sounds in the rhyme: ***French, China, Dutch.***
4. Note that most language names have the heaviest stress on the first syllable. Have the students find the exceptions (PapaGO, JapanESE, KorEan). Papago is a North American Indian language spoken in Arizona. The person noun is the same as the language name.
5. Rhyming vowel sounds are:

   /iy/ — Greek, speak, Portuguese, please
   /ə/ — Dutch, much
   /o/ — Papago, know
   /uw/ — too, do
   /ay/ — Thai, try

LEXICAL CHALLENGES

the language names

Loads of Languages

2.2

English, Latin, French, and Greek.
She's from China. What does she speak?

Turkish, Hindi, Finnish, Dutch.
He likes to speak them very much.

Urdu, Spanish, Portuguese.
Speak my language if you please.

Flemish, Welsh, and Papago.
How many languages do you know?

Russian, Polish, Japanese, too.
Do you speak them? Yes, I do.

Arabic, Wolof, Korean, Thai.
You can learn languages if you try.

NOTES FOR *Where's My Hat?*

ADDITIONAL ACTIVITIES 2.3

1. Make one copy with the prepositions whited out. Then make copies of the rhyme without the prepositions for the students. Play the tape or read the rhyme. The students fill in the blanks with the correct preposition.
2. Do the same as above, but white out the nouns instead of the prepositions.
3. Divide the rhyme into parts. Assign parts to pairs or small groups. Let them practice and then put it all together as a whole-class performance.
4. Hide a small object. Have the students ask yes/no questions using prepositions in order to find the object. For example, "Is it near the door?" Limit the number of questions to 15 or 20. The winner gets to hide the next object.
5. "What is it?" game. Describe the location of something in the room and then ask what it is. For example, "It's above the chalkboard, on the wall, behind me. What is it?"
6. Also see 2.4 "In, Out, On, and Off" for additional practice with prepositions.

LINGUISTIC NOTES

1. This rhyme features locative prepositions.
2. The rhythm of the rhyme requires contracted, reduced forms of *it's* and *isn't,* as well as *where's, can't, we're, we'll.*
3. Note that the rhymed pairs *door/floor* and *stool/pool* are spelled the same way but pronounced differently.
4. Rhyming vowel sounds are:

   /æ/ — hat, that
   /or/ — door, floor
   /uw/ — stool, pool
   /eyr/ — there, anywhere
   /i/ — him, gym
   /e/ — ten, then

LEXICAL CHALLENGES

floor stool swimming pool gym

Where's My Hat?

2.3

It's time to go.
Where's my hat?
Can anybody tell me that?

It's under the table.
It's near the door.
I saw it on the bathroom floor.

It isn't here.
It isn't there.
I can't find it anywhere.

It's on the desk,
beside the stool.
I think it's in the swimming pool.

It isn't here.
It isn't there.
I can't find it anywhere.

It's next to me.
It's next to him.
I think I saw it in the gym.

It's getting late.
Where's my hat?
Can anybody tell me that?

Come back at eight.
Come back at ten.
We're sure we'll find your hat by then.

NOTES FOR *In, Out, On, and Off*

ADDITIONAL ACTIVITIES 2.4

1. Make one copy with the prepositions whited out. Then make copies of the rhyme without the prepositions for the students. Play the tape or read the rhyme. The students fill in the blanks with the correct preposition.
2. For a greater challenge, do the same as above but do not play the tape or read the rhyme. Let the students fill in the blanks on their own.
3. Put a list of the vehicle nouns on the board and have the students use the appropriate prepositions with the nouns in a sentence of their own. Some suggestions of other vehicles: *bicycle, motorcycle, canoe, truck, skateboard, taxi.* With more advanced students, you may want to point out that *into* is sometimes used instead of *in, on to* instead of *on,* and *off of* instead of *off.*
4. Explain the idioms with "get" to the class. They can try using them in other short dialogues. You can also have them contribute other "get" idioms that they may know.
5. Also see 2.3 "Where's my Hat?" for more preposition practice.

LINGUISTIC NOTES

1. This rhyme features directional prepositions with "get" followed by a vehicle. The collocations are quite idiomatic, and so they have to be taught as idioms.
2. There are also other idiomatic expressions with "get" in the poem. They will need some explanation.

    Get in here!
    Get on the stick.
    Get out of line.
    Get out of here.
    Get off my back.

3. All the "get" verbs are in the imperative. You could have the students practice saying the rhyme with the negative ("don't get") and the "let's/let's not" forms.
4. Rhyming vowel sounds are:
    /ey/ — train, plane
    /ay/ — line, nine
    /e/ — jet, yet

LEXICAL CHALLENGES

in line stick waste back

In, Out, On, and Off

2.4

Get on the bus.
Get on the train.
You also must get on the plane.

Get in the car.
Get in line.
Get in here! It's half-past nine.

Get on the boat.
Get on the jet.
Get on the stick. You're not finished yet.

Get off the bus.
Get off the train.
You also must get off the plane.

Get out of the car.
Get out of line.
Get out of here. You're wasting my time.

Get off the boat.
Get off the jet.
Get off my back. I'm not finished yet.

NOTES FOR *My Favorite Place*

ADDITIONAL ACTIVITIES 2.5

1. Before working on the rhyme, have the students talk about their own "favorite places." Ask them to describe their places and how they feel about them.
2. Discuss the seasons, having the students compare the place they live or work now with their favorite places.
3. Divide the class into four groups and give each group one of the stanzas to read. After reading it one or two times this way, have the groups switch stanzas.

LINGUISTIC NOTES

1. This short rhyme has rather complex sentences beginning with the "I think," which is followed by a complement clause. Give special attention to the use of the coordinating conjunctions "and" and "but."
2. With the exception of one line, the rhythm in this rhyme is exclusively - /. Ask the students to find the line (It's the one beginning with *'n*). Ask them why *'cause* and *'n* are contracted and reduced.
3. Rhyming vowel sounds are:

   /aw / — tall, fall
   /o/ — snow, blow
   /eyr/ — care, there
   /ay/ — behind, mind

LEXICAL CHALLENGES

tree	flower	bloom	bird	fly
grew up	great	travel	distant	mind

My Favorite Place

2.5

I think, for me, my favorite place
is where the trees grow tall,
where flowers bloom in summertime,
and birds fly south in fall.

The winter can be very long,
and sometimes we have snow,
but still I love the icy cold
when winter winds will blow.

The springtime may be cold and gray,
but I don't really care
'cause I grew up in that great place,
'n my heart is always there.

I travel to some distant lands
and leave it all behind,
but still it is my favorite place,
a picture in my mind.

NOTES FOR *Around the Clock*

ADDITIONAL ACTIVITIES 3.1

1. Copy the rhyme and cut it into 13 couplets. Scramble and hand out the couplets to pairs of students. Read or play the rhyme as the students listen. Then the student pairs read their lines in the proper sequence.
2. After working on the rhyme, the students complete a chart of their own daily activities from 12 noon to 11 p.m. They could do one for a weekday and one for a weekend day.
3. Put clock faces with different times around the room with a sheet of paper under each. The students walk around and write one activity under each clock face.
4. For homework, have the students interview and write up the daily activity of another person, for example, "At one o'clock my mom eats lunch."

LINGUISTIC NOTES

1. The numbers from 1 to 12 are in this rhyme, along with the time expression "o'clock." This rhyme should be practiced before the next one, "Telling Time."
2. The rhyme contains several contractions: *there's, school's, 'most, homework's, 'til, I'll, it's, I'm, everyone's.* Be sure the students know what word is contracted.
3. There are eight different rhyming vowel sounds:

   /ay/ — high, sky, suppertime, fine, light, night
   /uw/ — through, do
   /ow/ — out, shout, doubt
   /o/ — home, poem
   /e/ — friend, ends, bed, head
   /ə/ — done, one, fun
   /iy/ — read, need
   /ey/ — away, day

4. There are quite a few potentially new words for lower proficiency level students.

LEXICAL CHALLENGES

sun	poem	dishes	doubt	dreaming
shine	program	homework	glad	out like a light
bright	suppertime	fun	rest	right away
sky	meal	busy	weary	brand new
shout				

Around the Clock

3.1

At 12 o'clock the hands are high.
The sun shines bright up in the sky.

At 1 o'clock my lunch is through.
It's afternoon. There's much to do.

At 2 o'clock school's 'most out,
and when it is, I'll run and shout.

At 3 o'clock I may go home,
or stay in class and write a poem.

At 4 o'clock I play with a friend,
or watch TV 'til the program ends.

At 5 o'clock it's suppertime.
Everyone's home and feeling fine.

At 6 o'clock the meal is done.
I wash the dishes one by one.

At 7 o'clock it's time to read
and study everything I need.

At 8 o'clock my homework's done.
No more books! Have some fun!

At 9 o'clock I'm tired out.
A busy day, without a doubt.

At 10 o' clock it's time for bed.
I'm glad to rest my weary head.

At 11 o'clock I'm out like a light,
sleeping and dreaming through the night.

At 6 o'clock I'm up right away
and ready for a brand new day.

Notes for *Telling Time*

Additional Activities — 3.2

1. As you read or play the tape, the students write the numerals in the margin near the spelled-out time, for example, they see and hear "four-fifteen" and write "4:15." Also point out the use of "of" for "to," as in "quarter of two," (lines 5 and 9).
2. Say one of the time expressions and have the students respond with an equivalent.
   For example: Teacher: four-fifteen
   Students: quarter past four
3. Give a dictation saying the time expression as the students write out the numerals.
4. Teach other time expressions, such as
   5:02 – five-oh-two; two (minutes) past five; two after five
   5:57 – five-fifty-seven; three (minutes) to six
   4:45 – (a) quarter to five; (a) quarter of five; four-forty-five
   Put several numerical times on the board. Point to one and ask a student to say all possible time expressions, for example,
   5:15 – (a) quarter past five; five-fifteen; (a) quarter after five
5. Go over the various ways people ask for the time, for example:
   Have you got the time?
   Do you have the time?
   What time is it, please?
   Can you tell me the time?

Linguistic Notes

1. Notice the use of the hyphen with compound numbers.
2. Rhyming vowel sounds are:

   /or/ – four, door
   /er/ – thirty, dirty
   /uw/ – two, do, you
   /iy/ – three, free
   /ay/ – nine, time
   /ey/ – day, say

Lexical Challenges

lock dirty free all the same during midnight fun

Telling Time

3.2

Four-fifteen or a quarter past four.
Don't forget to lock the door.

At half-past ten, it is ten-thirty.
Wash your hands. They're very dirty.

One forty-five is a quarter to two.
I just ate lunch, so what should I do?

Three oh five is five after three.
Time to go home. School's out. I'm free!

Eight thirty-five, twenty-five to nine.
It's all the same when you're telling time.

Twelve is noon if it's during the day.
At night it's "midnight" that you say.

Telling time is fun to do.
The way you tell it is up to you.

NOTES FOR *Our Day*

3.3

ADDITIONAL ACTIVITIES

1. Discuss daily routines with the students before doing the rhyme.
2. Have the students write in the margin what time they do the activities mentioned in the rhyme.
3. Divide the rhyme into parts. One group is "I" and the other is "she." Follow this with pairs practicing the two parts and presenting to the class.
4. Also see 3.1 "Around the Clock" and 3.2 "Telling Time."

LINGUISTIC NOTES

1. This rhyme uses the simple present for expressing habitual activities. Third person singular "-s" occurs throughout the rhyme, in contrast to first person singular.
2. The metric scheme in the rhyme is 4-3-4-3, but a few of the lines are tricky and can be read with a different stress pattern. Try saying the rhyme stressing "I" and "she," except for the very last "she," to show emphatic (contrasting) use of stress.
3. Rhyming vowel sounds are:

   /ay/ – nine, time
   /uw/ – too, school
   /ə/ – one, done
   /iy/ – see, university

LEXICAL CHALLENGES

drive math right university

Our Day

3.3

I get up at six o'clock.
She gets up at nine.
I eat breakfast right away.
She eats if there's time.

I wash my face and then my hands.
I think that she does, too.
I go out to get the bus.
She likes to drive to school.

I study math at eight o'clock.
She takes math at one.
I leave my books right in the class.
She brings hers home when done.

When I come home, I watch TV,
but she comes late, you see,
and she can do that 'cause she's
at the university.

Notes for *Attractive Opposites*

Additional Activities 4.1

1. Ask the students to circle all the adjectives in the rhyme.
2. Have the students put all the pairs of opposite adjectives on the board.
3. Ask the students to illustrate each of the third lines.
4. Have the students list several nouns in addition to those in the third lines, and ask them to write noun phrases with at least two adjectives before each noun.
5. See also 4.7 "Crazy Clothes" and 4.6 "The Rainbow" for additional practice with adjectives.

Linguistic Notes

1. This rhyme is loaded with adjectives, many of them opposites. As you work with the rhyme and some follow-up activities, keep in mind the general order of adjectives in English:

Poss Adj	Opinion	Size	Shape	Condition	Color	Origin	Noun
my	favorite	big	round	dirty	yellow	plastic	Frisbee

2. Many of these opposing pairs co-occur in a strict order. For example:
   hot and cold
   up and down
   young and old
   dead or alive
   back and forth
   Ask the students to think of other co-occurences that are usually said in only one way. For example: husband and wife, black and white, right or wrong, more or less, off and on.

3. Rhyming vowel sounds are:
   /ar/ — far, car
   /ow/ — down, town
   /uw/ — new, shoe
   /ey/ — late, gate
   /ay/ — alive, hive

Lexical Challenges

busy	tennis shoe	sad	swinging	wooden	gate	
fancy	plain	dead	alive	humming	hive	forth

Attractive Opposites

4.1

Tall and short,
near and far.
Old, expensive little car.

Hot and cold,
up and down.
Quiet, busy farming town.

Young and old,
old and new.
Black and yellow tennis shoe.

Happy and sad,
early and late.
Open, swinging wooden gate.

Plain and fancy,
dead or alive.
Humming black and yellow hive.

Back and forth,
up and down.
Opposites all over town.

NOTES FOR *Adjectives, Adjectives!*

ADDITIONAL ACTIVITIES 4.2

1. Ask the students to circle all the adjectives.
2. Have the students put all the adjectives on the board and then list all the opposites they can think of.
3. Ask the students to illustrate the rhyme.
4. Have the students list several nouns in addition to those in the rhyme and ask them to write noun phrases with one or two adjectives with each noun.
5. See also 4.7 "Crazy Clothes," 4.6 "The Rainbow," and 4.3 "Strange Scenes" for additional practice with adjectives.

LINGUISTIC NOTES

1. This rhyme is loaded with adjectives, many of them opposites. As you work with the rhyme and some follow-up activities, keep in mind the general order of adjectives in English:

Poss Adj	Opinion	Size	Shape	Condition	Color	Origin	Noun
my	favorite	big	round	dirty	yellow	plastic	Frisbee

2. Rhyming vowel sounds are:
   /iy/ — me, see, tea, sea, feet, street
   /ar/ — car, jar
   /eyr/ — hair, chair
   /a/ — dog, hog
   /i/ — ring, thing
   /o/ — boat, coat, old, cold

LEXICAL CHALLENGES

jelly jar	curly	hair	wooden	muddy	hog	diamond	ring
lemon	wavy	sea	boat	narrow	tree-lined		

Adjectives, Adjectives!

4.2

Adjectives, adjectives!
Look at me.
Adjectives, adjectives!
What do you see?

New black car, old jelly jar.
Curly brown hair, straight wooden chair.

Small white dog, big, muddy hog.
New diamond ring, any old thing.

Cold lemon tea, warm, wavy sea.
Expensive boat, cheap winter coat.

Pretty, narrow feet, tree-lined street.
Big and old, warm and cold.

Adjectives, adjectives!
Look at me.
Adjectives, adjectives!
What do you see?

Notes for *Strange Scenes*

Additional Activities 4.3

1. Assign the numbers from one to ten to ten different students or pairs. The students say the rhyme in sequence, each student/pair saying the lines with their number.
2. Have the class say the rhyme cumulatively, in the style of "The Twelve Days of Christmas." For example: There is **one** small black cat with boots, a coat, and hat.

   There is **one** small black cat with boots, a coat, and hat.
   There are **two** large brown dogs that are playing with a frog.

   There is **one** small black cat with boots, a coat, and hat.
   There are **two** large brown dogs that are playing with a frog.
   There are **three** gentle boys. They're quiet; there is no noise!
   etc.
3. Ask the students to circle the adjectives in the rhyme.

Linguistic Notes

1. There are many adjectives in this rhyme. See the notes for 4.2 "Adjectives, Adjectives!"
2. The noun phrases all have a quantifier (number). Quantifiers precede adjectives in a noun phrase. Normal order of a noun phrase is:

Determiner	**Quantifiers**	**Adjectives**	**Noun**
the	three	small, black	cats
my	several		
these	many		

3. Note the use of "there are" and "they are."
4. Rhyming vowel sounds are:

/æ/ — cat, hat	/or/ — boar, door
/a/ — dog, frog	/er/ — girls, curls
/oy/ — boys, noise	/eyr/ — bears, stairs
/e/ — gentlemen, hens	/iy/ — bees, tree
/i/ — pigs, wig	/o/ — poem, home

Lexical Challenges

boots	frog	noise	gentlemen	hen	purple	pig
pants	wig	boar	knocking	elephant	curl	polar bear
dancing	busy	bee	honey	tree	silly	poem

Strange Scenes

4.3

There is one small black cat
with boots, a coat, and hat.
There are two large brown dogs
that are playing with a frog.

There are three gentle boys.
They're quiet, there is no noise!
There are four gentlemen,
and five noisy hens.

There are six purple pigs
with jacket, pants, and wig.
There are just seven boars;
They are knocking at the door.

There are eight little girls
and elephants with curls.
There are nine polar bears,
and they're dancing on the stairs.

There are ten busy bees
with honey in a tree.
What a silly little poem,
and it's finished; let's go home.

NOTES FOR *Before My Eyes*

ADDITIONAL ACTIVITIES 4.4

1. Group the students in threes. Student A gets line 1 of each stanza; student B gets line 2, and Student C gets lines 3 and 4. They practice saying the lines in this way, and then say the rhyme for the entire class.
2. Practice saying the rhyme changing the "there is/are" statements to questions, for example: "Is there someone in the kitchen?" Change the very last line to "I would love to have one more."
3. List all the places mentioned in the rhyme and ask the students to individually write additional sentences for each place. For example, a student might write, "There's a mouse in the kitchen." Then have the students read their sentences to each other.

LINGUISTIC NOTES

1. This rhyme focuses on the "there is/are" construction. Note that "there is" is usually contracted in speech. There is also some elision with "there are" but it usually isn't written as a contracted form.
2. The rhyme easily works with question word order (see activity #2, above). You could also practice negative sentences and even negative questions, if you have worked with *some* and *any*.
3. Rhyming vowel sounds are:

   /aw / — hall, ball
   /ar/ — park, dark
   /iy/ — street, feet
   /i/ — ring, sing
   /or/ — store, more

LEXICAL CHALLENGES

hall	back yard	ball	concert	park	theater	whispering
dark	garden	across	upstairs	shuffling	handsome	stranger
diamond	ring	mystery	opera	chocolates		

Before My Eyes

4.4

There's someone in the kitchen.
There's someone in the hall.
There's someone in the back yard,
and he's playing with a ball.

There are people at the concert.
There are people in the park.
There are people in the theater,
and they're whispering in the dark.

There's a woman in the garden.
There's a man across the street.
There's dancing in the room upstairs.
I can hear the shuffling feet.

There's a dark and handsome stranger.
There's a missing diamond ring.
There's a mystery at the opera.
Are you listening to them sing?

There are teachers in the classroom.
There are shoppers in the store.
There are chocolates on the table,
and I'd like to have one more!

NOTES FOR *What's It Like?*

ADDITIONAL ACTIVITIES 4.5

1. List the stative verbs from the rhyme on the board: *feel, smell, taste, look.* Say a noun to a student and have them respond with a sentence using the noun and one of the stative verbs.
   For example: T: Candy.
   S: Candy tastes sweet.
   Some possible nouns, in addition to those in the rhyme: *cloud, flower, milk, wool, stars, beach, water, perfume.*
2. Have the students rewrite the rhyme replacing all the adjectives and nouns with their own words. Don't worry about the rhymes and rhythm.
3. Put single adjectives on separate sheets of poster paper around the room, and ask the students to write sentences under each adjective. For example, under "cool," a student might write, "Ice cream tastes cool on a hot day."

LINGUISTIC NOTES

1. The stative verbs in this rhyme are all linking verbs. They connect the subject noun with a complement, usually an adjective. Other common linking verbs are *go, get, seem, appear, grow, become, remain, turn, sound.*
2. *Feel, taste, smell,* and *sound* can also be non-linking and take an object. You could show examples to the students. For example, "I felt the earthquake," or "I smelled the rose."
3. Rhyming vowel sounds are:

   /ay/ — nice, ice
   /ey/ — great, cake
   /iy/ — sweet, treat
   /uw/ — cool, pool

LEXICAL CHALLENGES

snow	ice	smell	lovely	birthday cake	taste	sour
sweet	treat	cool	swimming	pool	roses	pizza
pickles	candy	pretzels	silly			

What's It Like?

4.5

That feels good.
That feels nice.
That feels cold as snow and ice.

That smells lovely.
That smells great.
I want a piece of birthday cake.

That tastes sour.
That tastes sweet.
I'd rather have a salty treat.

That looks good.
That looks cool.
Don't eat that in a swimming pool.

Sand feels good.
Silk feels nice.
Do they feel as cold as snow and ice?

Roses smell lovely.
Pizza smells great.
Want a piece of birthday cake?

Pickles taste sour.
Candy tastes sweet,
and pretzels make a salty treat.

Your clothes look good.
Your shoes look cool,
but they'd look silly in a swimming pool.

Notes for *The Rainbow*

Additional Activities 4.6

1. Have the students discuss or write about their favorite color. Some leading questions: Why do you like it? What do you own that is that color?
2. List the colors of the rainbow on the board or on pieces of paper around the room (the rhyme follows the order, ROYGBIV). The students list as many things as possible that fit under each color.
3. Discuss rainbows and stories and legends from various cultures. How do you say "rainbow" in other languages?
4. Have the students write an original rhyme about a rainbow.
5. Brainstorm other color words (pink, brown, rose, etc.) and words that describe colors (*bright, pale, light, dark, deep,* etc.)

Linguistic Notes

1. This rhyme is very simple, grammatically. There are only two complete sentences (ask the students to find them). All other lines are simply descriptive phrases.
2. There is only one rhyming vowel sound: /uw/ — too, blue, you. These words are repeated in each stanza. There is also an example of /yuw/ — view.

Lexical Challenges

rainbow	paint(ed)	view	pale	light	indigo
violet	disappear	catch	bright	sky	magic
air					

The Rainbow

4.6

Rainbow painted on the sky,
seven colors there to view —
Red and orange, yellow too,
beautiful green and pale light blue,
indigo, violet just for you.

Catch the colors in your hand.
Paint them on a bright blue sky —
Red and orange, yellow too,
beautiful green and pale light blue,
indigo, violet just for you.

Magic colors in the air.
Watch them slowly disappear —
Red and orange, yellow too,
beautiful green and pale light blue,
indigo, violet just for you.

NOTES FOR *Crazy Clothes*

ADDITIONAL ACTIVITIES 4.7

1. There may be a lot of new words in this rhyme, so it is important that the students know the vocabulary of clothing before they begin.
2. Assign each stanza to a different group. Allow them time to practice and work on pronunciation. Then they perform the stanza for the class.
3. Bring in colored markers and have each group draw a person or people wearing the clothes described in their group's stanza.
4. Practice the poem at different speeds – very slow, then very fast.
5. Have the students become fashion designers. They draw pictures of some crazy clothes and then share their drawings with their classmates describing the clothes.
6. The students bring crazy clothes to class and have a fashion show. In pairs, one student acts as the announcer while the other models the clothes.

LINGUISTIC NOTES

1. There are several examples of noun phrases that include color adjectives and adjectives that modify colors. See the note about adjective ordering in 4.2 "Adjectives, Adjectives!"
2. This is a highly rhythmic rhyme, almost like a chant at a sporting event. Chant it that way.
3. Rhyming vowel sounds are:

   /ey/ — day, hey
   /o/ — coat, boat
   /or/ — shorts, courts
   /e/ — belt, felt
   /er/ — shirt, skirt
   /ay/ — tie, guy
   /a/ — socks, box

LEXICAL CHALLENGES

crazy	boat	silver	shirt	tie	vinyl
wear	scarf	belt	long	striped	hot pink
bright	cotton	diamond	light	pants	pajamas
sneakers	shorts	earrings	gold	guy	polka-dotted
purple	basketball	felt	vest	silk	miniskirt
leather	courts	jacket	pink	blouse	shoes
plastic	shiny	dark	paisley	nylon	box
boot					

Crazy Clothes

4.7

Crazy clothes, crazy clothes!
Wear them every day.
Crazy clothes, crazy clothes!
Hey! Hey! Hey!

Bright red sneakers,
and a purple leather coat.
Yellow plastic boots
that you wear in a boat.

Polka-dotted scarf
and some black cotton shorts.
Where can you wear them?
On a basketball court.

Hot pink pajamas
with a shiny silver belt.
White diamond earrings
and a hat made of felt.

Green and yellow jacket
with a dark brown shirt.
Long black boots
and an orange miniskirt.

Light gold vest
and a pink paisley tie.
Red striped pants.
Would you look at that guy!

A fine silk blouse
and some cheap nylon socks.
Old vinyl shoes
that you keep in a box.

Crazy clothes, crazy clothes!
Wear them every day.
Crazy clothes, crazy clothes!
Hey! Hey! Hey!

NOTES FOR *Move Your Body*

ADDITIONAL ACTIVITIES 5.1

1. Have the students review words for parts of the body. One student can draw an outline of a body on the board, and the others can call out the names for the parts. Add others that the students might not know.
2. Have the students work in pairs and give each other a series of commands to do things.
3. In two minutes or less, each student teaches the class how to do something. Have the students write it out before they try it.
4. Set up a three-part reading using different body parts, following this pattern:

   Student A to student C: Touch your nose.
   Student B to student C: What are you doing?
   Student C: I'm touching my nose.

5. This rhyme lends itself to "Simon Says." When the leader says "Don't" the followers don't move. Those who do are out.
6. Also see 5.2 "Head to 5.3 Toe" and "Your Eyes to See" for more work with the lexicon of the body.

LINGUISTIC NOTES

1. The verbs are all in the imperative mood. You could practice the negative by having them say "Don't touch your nose," etc.
2. Another variation is to have each line begin with the more polite "Would you please."
3. Rhyming vowel sounds are:

   /i/ — hips, fingertips
   /iy/ — knees, please
   /o/ — toes, rows
   /æ/ — back, track
   /or/ — door, snore
   /e/ — pen, ag<u>ai</u>n

LEXICAL CHALLENGES

touch	reach	bend	toes	step	snore
shake	sky	knees	perfect	forward	jump
hips	fingertips	politely	row	track	grab

Move Your Body

5.1

Touch your nose.
Shake your hips.
Reach the sky with your fingertips.

Move your head.
Bend your knees.
Ask politely, and say "please."

Turn around.
Touch your toes.
Put your desks in perfect rows.

One step forward.
One step back.
Run three times around the track.

Open the window.
Close the door.
Go to sleep, but do not snore.

Jump four times.
Grab your pen.
Then sit down and study again.

Notes for *From Head to Toe*

Additional Activities 5.2

1. Have one student draw a large representation of a body on the board. The other students call out the names for parts of the body, and the person at the board labels the drawing.
2. In pairs, one student says the lines of the rhyme while the other points to the body part as it is read. They reverse roles.
3. One person can call out the name of a part of the body while the class responds in unison by pointing to the part. The leader can intentionally try to trick the others by pointing to the wrong part.

Linguistic Notes

1. There are three locative prepositions: ***on, below, under.*** You could add others such as b***eneath, between, above, over, in,*** and have the students practice using them as they describe the locations of parts of the body.
2. Rhyming vowel sounds are:
   /iy/ — see, these, feet, seat
   /o/ — toes, nose
   /ow/ — mouth, south
   /i/ — lips, fingertips, shin, chin
3. Note the /sh/ and /ch/ consonant contrast in *shin* and *chin.*

Lexical Challenges

body	ear	eye	touch	ankle	chin
toe	mouth	lip	fingertip	shin	floor

From Head to Toe

5.2

Parts of the body you can see.
Parts of the body,
look at these:

Head and toes, head and toes.
On your face,
you'll find your nose.

Ears and mouth, ears and mouth.
On your head,
east, west, and south.

Eyes and lips, eyes and lips.
Touch them all
with your fingertips.

Ankle and shin, ankle and shin.
Both are far
below your chin.

Legs and feet, legs and feet.
They're on the floor,
under your seat.

Notes for *Your Eyes to See*

Additional Activities 5.3

1. Go over the lexicon of the body before working with the rhyme. Put all the terms on the board and have the students try to describe the location and function of the body part.

2. After doing the rhyme a few times, give the students copies with all the body words whited out, and have them fill them in.

3. Have pairs of students practice this pattern:

   Student A: What do you do with your eyes?
   Student B: You use your eyes to see.
   Student A: What do you do with your nose?
   Student B: You use your nose to smell.
   etc.

4. Another pattern to try:

   Student A: What are your eyes for?
   Student B: Your eyes are for seeing.
   Student A: What is your nose for?
   Student B: Your nose is for smelling.
   etc.

Linguistic Notes

1. The pattern, "Your ____ to ____," is an abbreviated poetic pattern, and not, of course, a normal sentence. The last stanza has a more normal sentence structure. You could rephrase the other stanzas to fit this pattern, for example, "Your eyes to see" becomes "Your eyes see."

2. All the lines use the impersonal "your," which could be replaced by "our" or "the." The rhyme could be varied by using personal pronouns: *my, his, her.*

3. Rhyming vowel sounds are:

   /i,i/ — singing, ringing
   /e,i/ — bending, mending
   /iy, i/ — meaning, cleaning
   /a, i/ — walking, talking

Lexical Challenges

eye	ring	back	heart	brain	point	eyelid
smell	neck	lean	beat	feed	elbow	vocal cord
ear	step	grab	lung	kidney	bend	
reach	knee	finger	breathe	clean	eyebrow	
mouth	bend	mend	shoulder	finger	arch	

Your Eyes to See

5.3

Your eyes to see.
Your nose to smell.
Your ears to hear the singing.
Your hand to reach.
Your mouth to speak.
Your ears to hear the ringing.

Your neck to turn.
Your feet to step.
Your knees to do the bending.
Your back to lean.
Your hand to grab.
Your fingers to do the mending.

Your heart to beat.
Your lungs to breathe.
Your shoulders to raise for meaning.
Your brain to think.
Your mouth to feed.
Your kidneys to do the cleaning.

Your finger points.
Your elbow bends.
Your legs to do the walking.
Your eyebrows arch.
Your eyelids close.
Your vocal cords for talking.

NOTES FOR *You Can Do Anything*

ADDITIONAL ACTIVITIES 6.1

1. Ask the students to read each stanza and write the occupation or activity being described. For each occupation/activity, the students then write 3-5 sentences about other things that person might do, for example:

   Stanza 1: A businessperson
   A businessperson calls many people from the office.
   A businessperson travels to different places.

2. In pairs or individually, the students brainstorm as many occupations as they can think of. Write them on the board. Each student chooses one and prepares a poster or sheet of paper with a picture related to the occupation and 5-8 sentences with different verbs describing the activities that a person in such an occupation does. Hang the pictures around the room to create an "occupation gallery."

3. Have the students write about what they want to do when they're adults. For adult students, ask them to write about a new career and why they would want to have such a career.

4. Ask the students to describe in detail what people in different occupations wear, or show pictures of people to the students and see if they can guess the occupations from the way people are dressed.

LINGUISTIC NOTES

1. The basic rhythm of this rhyme is very simple, two stressed syllables to a line, but there are variations in the number of syllables. It's a good rhyme for saying the lines and reducing the unstressed syllables. The last stanza, however, has four stressed syllables to a line.

2. The rhyme talks about what people do; hence the natural verb tense is simple present.

3. Note that in the last stanza, all the lines rhyme with /uw/. Other vowel rhymes are:

   /ay/ — tie, guy
   /uw/ — boots, toot
   /a/ — socks, blocks
   /æ/ — cap, that
   /e/ — pen, then

LEXICAL CHALLENGES

shirt	guy	boots	shorts	basketball	leather	computer
jacket	gloves	cycle	cotton	shoots	cap	whole
suit	helmet	toot	socks	blocks	baseball	dreams
tie	pants	T-shirt				

You Can Do Anything

6.1

Shirt and jacket,
suit and tie,
look at him,
a business guy.

Gloves and helmet,
pants and boots,
a woman on a cycle,
Toot! Toot! Toot!

T-shirt, shorts
and cotton socks,
a basketball player
who shoots and blocks.

Leather glove
and cotton cap,
she plays baseball.
Look at that!

New computer,
books and pen,
he studies all night,
even after ten.

All these things that people do,
morning and night, the whole day through.
You can do them. It's up to you.
Choose your dreams and wishes, too.

Notes for *Things I Like to Do*

Additional Activities

6.2

1. Ask the students to list all the things the person in the rhyme likes to do. After each item, they write their own personal response.
   For example: I like to play tennis, too.
   I don't like to play tennis.
   They can then pair up and share their answers.

2. Have the students write or talk about their own favorite things to do.

3. Call out a few "things to do" from the rhyme and ask a student to mime the activity. This can be combined with a "Simon Says" activity.
   For example: Teacher: Simon says "Play some tennis."
   Students mime playing tennis.
   Teacher: Ride your bike.
   Students do not mime. (Those who do are "out.")

Linguistic Notes

1. The verbs are in the imperative form. Practice saying the verb phrases as negative imperatives: Don't play tennis, etc., or "Let's not play tennis," etc.

2. To form sentences with infinitives, go through the verb phrases preceding each one with "I like to. . . "

3. Note the idiomatic collocations with the verbs *take, ride, do, have.* The students can try to form other collocations with the verbs, such as *take a nap, take a bus, take a shower, take a break,* etc.

4. Rhyming vowel sounds are:

   /ay/ – bike, hike
   /uw/ – school, pool
   /e/ – friend, mend
   /iy/ – dreams, moonbeams
   /ey/ – away, day

Lexical Challenges

tennis	hike	sew	mall	moonbeam
ride	swim	sock	sweet	right away
bike	pool	mend	dream	smile
bath	favor	poem	skies	brand-new

Things I Like to Do

6.2

Play some tennis.
Ride my bike.
Take a bath,
or take a hike.
Do my homework
after school.
Take a swim
in a swimming pool.

Do a favor
for a friend.
Sew my sock;
I like to mend.
Write a poem.
Read a book.
Go to the mall,
and have a look.

Go to bed.
Have sweet dreams
under the skies
with bright moonbeams.
Wake up early,
right away.
Smile and sing;
it's a brand-new day.

Notes for *Different Likes*

Additional Activities

6.3

1. Have the students make a list of their own favorite things to do. They can then share them in pairs or small groups.
2. Ask the students to list all the "likes" mentioned in the rhyme. In pairs they ask each other if they like those things. They can answer with short or long responses, according to your directions.
   For example: Line 1: I like science.
   Student A: Do you like science?
   Student B: Yes I do. or Yes, I like science. It's my favorite class.
3. Say the rhyme to the students and ask them to say the last line of each stanza.
   For example:
   Teacher: I like science. I like math. I do it before I take my. . .
   Students: Bath!

Linguistic Notes

1. Each stanza has a different subject pronoun, in the usual order: I, you, he, she, we, they.
2. The verb is in the present simple. It requires third-person singular subject-verb agreement.
3. Rhyming vowel sounds are:

   /æ/ – math, bath, bats, that
   /iy/ – tea, history, dreams, cream
   /i/ – gym, rim
   /uw/ – school, cool

Lexical Challenges

science	tiger	soccer	touch	chocolate
math	bat	gym	rim	cake
bath	spider	shoot	cool	mint
history	crab	basket	dream	ice cream

Different Likes

6.3

I like science.
I like math.
I do it before I take my bath.

You like coffee.
You like tea.
Time to study history!

He likes tigers.
She likes bats.
Spiders, crabs, imagine that!

She likes soccer.
He likes gym.
Shoot a basket! Touch the rim!

We like English.
We like school.
Learning things is pretty cool.

They like nighttime.
They like dreams
of chocolate cake and mint ice cream.

Notes for *The Things That People Do*

Additional Activities 6.4

1. Have the students underline or circle all the verbs in the rhyme. Ask them to write two original sentences with each verb. They can exchange papers and share and/or correct the sentences.

2. One student leaves the room. The others choose one of the occupations in the rhyme. The student returns, and in turn, each student tells one thing that they do. The returning student identifies the occupation.
   For example: Student A: I lend money.
   Student B: You're a banker.
   Student C: I create a dish.
   Student B: You're a chef.
   This can be done with other occupations not in the rhyme.

3. Play "10 Questions." One student chooses an occupation, and the others ask yes/no questions. They try to guess the first student's occupation with ten or fewer questions.

4. In pairs or individually, the students brainstorm as many occupations as they can think of. Write them on the board. Each student chooses one and prepares a poster or sheet of paper with a picture related to the occupation and 5-8 sentences with different verbs describing the activities that a person in such an occupation does. Hang the pictures around the room to create an "occupation gallery."

Linguistic Notes

1. All the main verb phrases are in the simple present, third-person singular.

2. Most of the verbs are transitive. Go through the rhyme with the students looking for objects for the verbs. Identify the verbs that don't take an object. Note that some verbs do not have explicit objects in the rhyme, but are usually transitive *(sell, plan, plow).*

3. Rhyming vowel sounds are:

   /i/ — pills, ills, dish, fish
   /uw/ — too, two
   /æ/ — class, pass, plans, lands
   /ow/ — plows, cows
   /ay/ — crime, time

Lexical Challenges

pill	prepare	plan	plant	lawyer	chef	vegetable
patient	pass	client	seed	court	create	spaghetti
ills	travel	distant	plow	crime	dish	egg
lend	agent	land	chore	law	cook	fish
busy	sell	farmer	milk	require	sauce	

The Things That People Do

6.4

A doctor helps the sick.
A doctor gives them pills.
A doctor helps the patients
feel better from their ills.

A banker counts the money.
A banker lends it, too.
A banker has a busy day
and works from nine to two.

A teacher prepares lessons.
A teacher comes to class.
A teacher teaches many things
and helps the students pass.

A travel agent sells.
A travel agent plans.
A travel agent helps the clients
go to distant lands.

A farmer plants the seeds.
A farmer also plows.
A farmer does his daily chores
and has to milk the cows.

A lawyer goes to court.
A lawyer knows the crime.
A lawyer studies laws
that require lots of time.

A chef prepares the food.
A chef creates a dish.
A chef cooks sauce and vegetables,
spaghetti, eggs, and fish.

NOTES FOR *What'll Ya Have?*

ADDITIONAL ACTIVITIES 7.1

1. Make a copy of the rhyme with the food and drink items whited out. Have the students fill in the blanks. You can also have them do this as you say or play the rhyme.
2. The students make a list of their favorite foods and talk about them in pairs or small groups. They should also try to use the appropriate quantifying words.
3. Role-play a supermarket scene, or two people planning a shopping list.
4. Have a snack and drink party. Plan who will bring what. Make sure there's a variety of items. The students bring in the items and name them as they show them to the class.
   For example: I brought a bag of potato chips.
   I have a liter of Coke.
   I 've got a bunch of grapes.
   I've got a box of crackers/ slices of cheese/ jar of olives/ can of sardines.

LINGUISTIC NOTES

1. This rhyme is loaded with food and quantity vocabulary. You may need to precede the rhyme with a class or two focused on the vocabulary in the rhyme.
2. This rhyme features partitives and measure words. The partitives occur with noncount nouns. Identify all the noncount nouns and have the students make sentences without the partitive, for example, "I'd like some coffee."
3. The partitive words can be pluralized. Go through all the expressions putting "two" in front of each one. Watch out for "dozen."
4. Every two lines rhyme. The rhyming vowel sounds are:

   /iy/ — tea, pastry, peas, please
   /ay/ — wine, fine, thyme, lime, rice, nice
   /ey/ — cake, take, grapes, tapes
   /e/ — bread, said
   /uw/ — soup, scoop, shoes, use
   /æ/ — jam, lamb
   /a/ — pop, shop
   /o/ — tomatos, potatoes
   /eyr/ — air, dare

LEXICAL CHALLENGES

sugar	lettuce	dish	pinch	plate	eggs	stack	socks	gulp
pastry	loaf	scoop	touch	rice	tomato	roll	shoes	air
juice	bread	cube	thyme	tortilla	loaf	film	glasses	dare
wine	clove	jar	slice	bottle	bread	can	sip	
pie	garlic	jam	lemon	beer	bag	peas	juice	
cake	bowl	side	lime	pop	potato	stick	ice cream	
pizza	chili	beef	order	wine	bunch	gum	chili pepper	
head	soup	lamb	beans	dozen	grape	pair	videotape	

What'll Ya Have?

7.1

A cup of coffee, a cup of tea,
a cup of sugar in French pastry.
A glass of juice, a glass of wine,
a glass of water is just fine.

A piece of pie, a piece of cake,
a piece of pizza is what I'll take.
A head of lettuce, a loaf of bread,
a clove of garlic is what I said.

A bowl of chili, a bowl of soup,
a dish of ice cream, want a scoop?
A cube of sugar, a jar of jam,
a side of beef, a leg of lamb.

A pinch of salt, a touch of thyme,
a slice of lemon and a slice of lime.
An order of beans, a plate of rice,
a few tortillas would be nice.

A bottle of beer, a bottle of pop,
a bottle of wine from the shop.
A dozen eggs and a pound of tomatos,
a loaf of bread, and a bag of potatoes.

A bunch of bananas, a bunch of grapes,
a stack of cassettes and some videotapes.
A roll of film, a can of peas,
a stick of gum if you say please.

A pair of socks, a pair of shoes,
a pair of glasses I will use.
A sip of juice, a gulp of air,
a chili pepper if you dare!

NOTES FOR *In a Diner*

ADDITIONAL ACTIVITIES 7.2

1. Assign a different line to each student. They read the rhyme one line at a time without losing the beat.
2. Have pairs practice the rhyme as a conversation. They present it to the class.
3. Discuss eating out. Talk about favorite places and things to eat. Compare dining customs.

LINGUISTIC NOTES

1. These lines are somewhat conversational. The rhyme starts with a very common feature of spoken English: omission of the first parts of the sentence. "Want to" is also reduced and elided to "wanna."
2. Notice the various contractions.
3. This rhyme has a lot of phrases with a --/ pattern:

   `-    - /  - -   /    - - / - - /`
   Want to **sit**, at the **count**er, or **sit** in a **booth?**

4. Rhyming vowel sounds are:

   /iy/ — me, trees
   /o/ — Coke, joke
   /ey/ — day, okay

LEXICAL CHALLENGES

counter	view	tree	really	joke	hard
booth	river	sandwich	salad	waitress	tip
window	hill				

In a Diner

7.2

Want to sit at the counter or sit in a booth?
Either is fine with me.
Let's sit by the window, the one with the view
of the river, the hills, and the trees.

I'm having a sandwich. What about you?
I think I'll have a Coke.
You really should eat better than that:
Salad and water, no joke!

Here comes our waitress, she really is quick.
She works very hard through the day.
Let's leave a nice tip for all that she's done.
I've got it. Is that okay?

NOTES FOR *In a Deli*

ADDITIONAL ACTIVITIES 7.3

1. Go over the vocabulary, and if necessary, an explanation of what a deli is.
2. Assign one line to each student. They read it through line by line without missing the beat.
3. Assign the rhyme to triads. Each person reads one stanza. They perform it for the others.
4. Discuss vegetarianism and other kinds of food preferences and prohibitions.
5. If possible, visit and have lunch at a deli.

LINGUISTIC NOTES

1. *There is/isn't* occurs frequently in this rhyme. It could lead to a question/answer practice along the lines of:

   Student A: Is there lamb in this deli?
   Student B: Yes, there is.
   Student A: Is there ice cream?
   Student B: No, there isn't.

2. Rhyming vowel sounds are:

   /ow/ – about, doubt
   /æ/ – ham, lamb
   /ə/ – bun, vegetari<u>an</u>

LEXICAL CHALLENGES

meat	mustard	Swiss	ham	glad
cheese	rye	wheat bread	special	sandwich
dream	doubt	turkey	spicy	bun
hot pastrami	corned beef	beef	lamb	vegetarian

In a Deli

7.3

Look at all that meat and cheese.
It's all I dream about.
A hot pastrami, mustard, rye –
The best in town, no doubt.

There's corned beef, Swiss, and wheat bread, too.
There's turkey, beef, and ham.
There's even a special of the day.
It looks like spicy lamb.

I'm glad you're happy with this place,
and your sandwich on a bun,
but there isn't much that I can eat.
I'm a vegetarian!

NOTES FOR *In a Fancy Restaurant*

ADDITIONAL ACTIVITIES 7.4

1. Assign one line to each student. Go through the rhyme one line at a time, keeping up the rhythm.
2. Assign the rhyme to triads. Have them practice it as a conversation between a waiter and two diners. Then they perform for the class.
3. The students write and act out their own "fancy restaurant" scene.

LINGUISTIC NOTES

1. Notice the use of "that" and "it" as subjects in the sentence. Provide the students with additional sentences commenting on the fancy restaurant scene. They can change the "It" sentences to "That was" sentences. Some examples:

It's a very nice place.	That was a very nice place.
It's very expensive.	That was very expensive.
It's a celebration .	That was a celebration.
It's very fancy.	That was very fancy.
It's delicious.	That was delicious.
It's a very nice wine.	That was a very nice wine.

2. Rhyming vowel sounds are:

/uw/ — two, you
/iyr/ — here, year
/ ə , iy/ — money, honey

LEXICAL CHALLENGES

suit perfectly	suggest	shock	night out	celebrate
wine list	really	dish	money	honey
cabernet	menu	heck		

In a Fancy Restaurant

7.4

Good evening, sir. Good evening, ma'am.
A table in back for two?
That would suit us perfectly.
How very kind of you.

The wine list's on the table there.
Would you pass it over here?
I think I'll choose a cabernet.
Can you suggest a year?

Sixty-eight was very good.
So was seventy-two.
That's really all that I can say.
The choice is up to you.

Have you seen the menu yet?
It may be a shock to you.
One hundred dollars for a dish,
and some as high as two.

Oh, what the heck! It's our night out.
It may cost lots of money.
Forget the cost, we'll celebrate
for me and for my honey!

NOTES FOR *Another Meal Out*

ADDITIONAL ACTIVITIES 7.5

1. Discuss various ways to prepare food, and healthy and unhealthy eating habits. Look at the food items in the rhyme and have the students rate them as healthy or not.
2. Have the students work in groups to practice and put on the rhyme as a conversation.
3. Create a dialogue for a possible conversation in a local restaurant.
4. Have the students research the nutritional values of various foods and bring in the results for a discussion.

LINGUISTIC NOTES

1. Notice the contracted "would" in "I'd like to" and "I'd love to." Have the students look at the rhyme and make more sentences with "I'd like to."
   For example: I'd like to have a sandwich.
   I'd like to have a salad.
   I'd like to have a baked potato.
2. Rhyming vowel sounds are:

   /i/ — fish, dish
   /ay/ — fried, tried, while, smile

LEXICAL CHALLENGES

sandwich	meal	baked	decide	smile	pants
fish	dish	fried	really	dessert	fit
suggest	potato	salad	pleasant		

Another Meal Out

7.5

I think I'll have a sandwich.
I'd like to try the fish.
Can you suggest a meal for me –
a different sort of dish?

Please give me some potatoes.
I'd like one baked, not fried.
You ought to get the salad here –
the best I've ever tried.

I haven't yet decided.
Could you come back in a while?
He's really such a pleasant man –
a waiter with a smile.

Look at those desserts!
I'd love to try them all.
My friend, if you do that,
your pants won't fit at all.

A Brief Note on Pronunciation

As we speak English, some of the syllables in a word, or some of the words in a phrase or sentence, will be spoken with more force than others:

FOUR of the **SYL**lables in this **SENT**ence are **LOUD.**

We automatically turn up the volume as we utter stressed (loud) syllables. At the same time, as the syllable becomes louder, it also tends to become longer in duration and higher in pitch.

SIX of the **SYL**lables in this **SENT**ence are **LOUD, LONG** and **HIGH.**

In English, stressed syllables tend to crowd out the other syllables, which are consequently spoken quietly and quickly. In the word "syllable" (**syl**-la-ble), the first syllable is stressed, and the other two syllables are not stressed. As this happens, there is a strong tendency for the unstressed vowels to change into an "uh" sound, a vowel sound called "schwa." This process is called **reduction,** and it occurs in most multi-syllable words and in most long phrases and sentences.

Now compare and say:

/
noun

/ \
pronoun

_ /
pronounce

_ \ \ / _
pronunciation

The first word, "noun," is a single-syllable word. It has **primary stress (/)** because every word spoken in isolation (not as part of a longer phrase or sentence) must have a strong, or primary stress, on one syllable. The next word, "pronoun," is stressed heavily on the first syllable, but the second syllable is not completely reduced. It still has some stress, and the vowel is not reduced to "uh." This is called **secondary stress.**
In the verb "pronounce," the vowel in the first syllable is reduced to the point of becoming "uh." This example shows that when stress is weak, the vowel tends to lose its identity to become the short, weak, unstressed schwa.

Now look at the word "pronunciation." The syllable "a" receives the primary stress, but "nun" also receives some stress – secondary stress. "Pro" and "tion" are spoken quickly and quietly with only weak stress, and the vowels are reduced to "uh."

In summary, words can have three levels of stress: primary (/), secondary (\), and weak (_).

When several words are strung together as a phrase or sentence, this group of words acts somewhat like a single word. One syllable in the group will receive heavier stress than the other syllables in the group. In a normal statement sentence, the final stressed syllable in the sentence will receive the heaviest stress. This is **major phrase/ sentence stress,** marked with a double slash (//).

However, major sentence stress does not always occur on the final stressed syllable in a sentence. This happens when the speaker wants to focus attention on some other word in the sentence for emphasis or contrast. In the rhyme "Our Day," the first word in the sentence gets major sentence stress because the rhyme is contrasting "I" and "she:"

//   /   /
I get up at six o'clock.

//   /   /
She gets up at nine.

Finally, **intonation** is also influenced by stress. Intonation is the way voices go up (high) and down (low) as we speak. It's like melody in music. In general, intonation is high on stressed syllables and lower on unstressed syllables, and it usually falls at the end of a statement and rises at the end of a yes/no question.

Would you please repeat this poem?

Say it twice and then go home.

Indexes

Grammatical Features

Topics

Indexes

Vowel Rhymes

Other Books from Pro Lingua on

Pronunciation and Speaking

Pronunciation Activities: Vowels in Limericks. Middle school, high school, adult. Advanced beginners to low intermediate. Pronunciation is made fun and effective using 16 comical limericks, each one focused on one vowel sound (Adam, Billy, Gus, Brooke, Paul, etc.) illustrated by witty cartoons. Several varied activities reinforce the vowel sound. Students also practice rhythm, stress, and phrasing as they recite the limericks.
Cassette available.

Pronunciation Card Games. A photocopyable resource book. Middle school to adult. Beginner to low intermediate. 16 games using index cards constructed with the photocopyable pages in the book. You need scissors and paste. The games work on difficult vowel and consonant sounds, syllabification, stress, and intonation.

Celebrating American Heroes. All ages and proficiency levels. 13 brief plays about significant historical figures from Sacagawea to Cesar Chavez. They are designed for reading aloud dramatically. In each play there are a few main characters and a chorus that comments and advises by chanting about the actions of the heroes. Everybody participates.
Teacher's Guide (photocopyable) and Cassette available.

Story Cards. All ages, advanced beginners to advanced. The students get a card, study it, and then tell the story to a partner or to the class. Excellent guided speaking practice that is also fun and informative. Three different sets are available:

North American Indian Tales. 48 animal stories from tribes across the continent. Color illustrations of each story.

Aesop's Fables. 48 classic fables known the world over. Color illustrations.

The Tales of Nasreddin Hodja. 40 stories about the legendary Turkish humorist with an incomparable sense of humor and ageless common sense. Smiles, laughs, and wonderful illustrations.

Stranger in Town. High school to adult. Intermediate to advanced proficiency. A dramatic play in four acts for reading aloud or even for a class performance. 18 characters weave through the play as the stranger with a past arrives in town and takes up residence and responsibility. It's an allegory for the process of learning and cultural adjustment.
Cassette available.